Number Puzzles

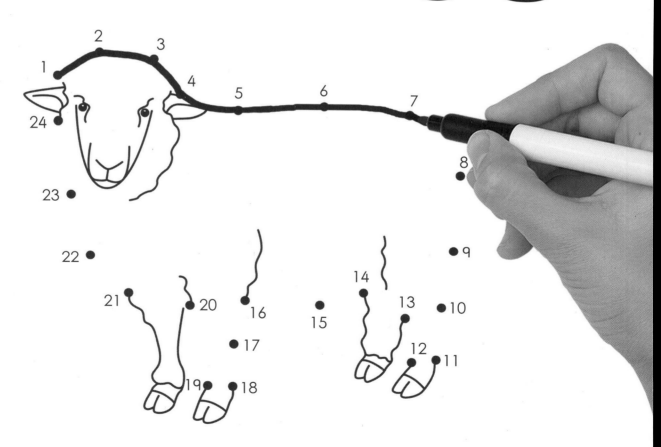

priddy books
big ideas for little people

Count each group of objects, trace over the numbers, and then draw a line to the groups they match.

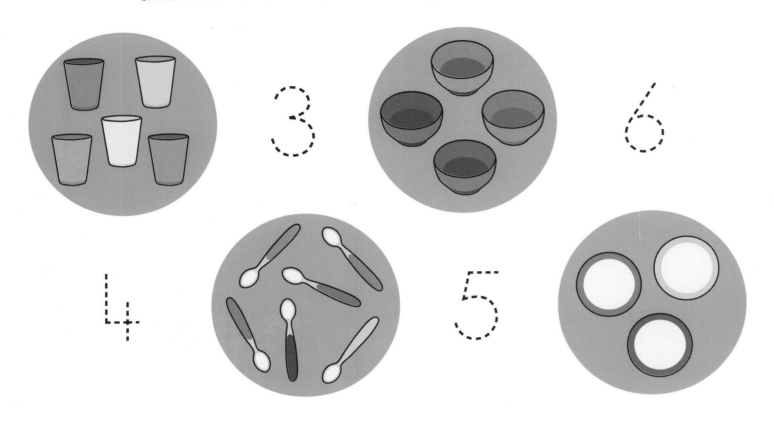

3

6

4

5

How many flowers?

Circle the T-shirt with the most flowers.

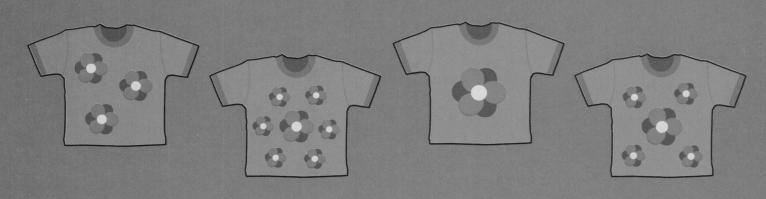

What color are the T-shirts?

Count the objects in each row, and then write the totals in the boxes.

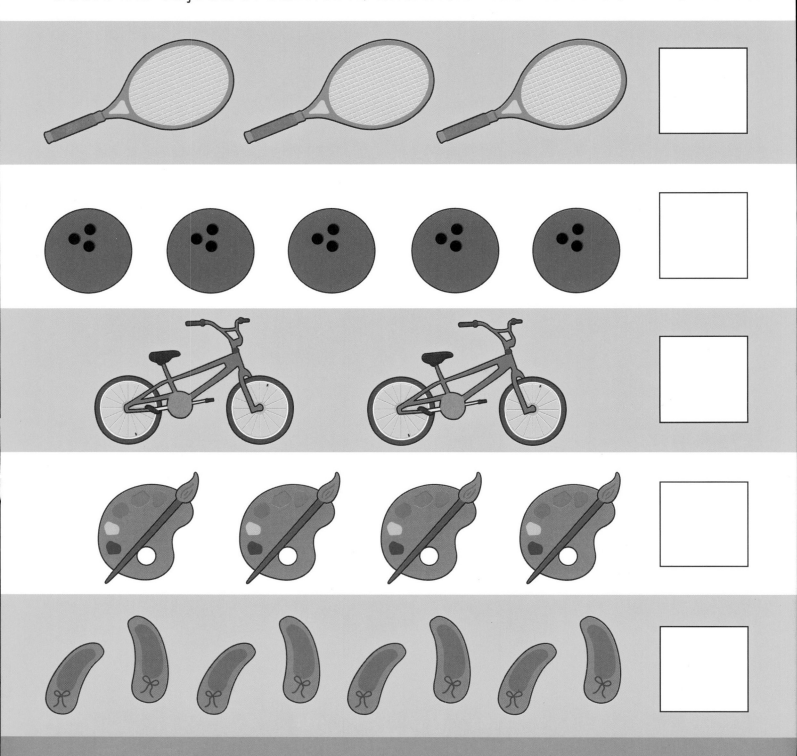

Look closely at the pirate scene, and then answer the counting questions below.

How many colorful parrots can you count?

How many eye patches can you count?

How many pirate hats can you count?

How many pirates are holding cutlasses?

Which pirate is wearing a green shirt?

Which bracelet has the most jewels? Circle your answer.

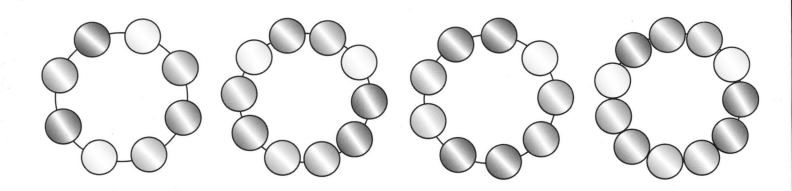

Connect the dots to draw the princess tiara. Why not color in the tiara once your picture is complete?

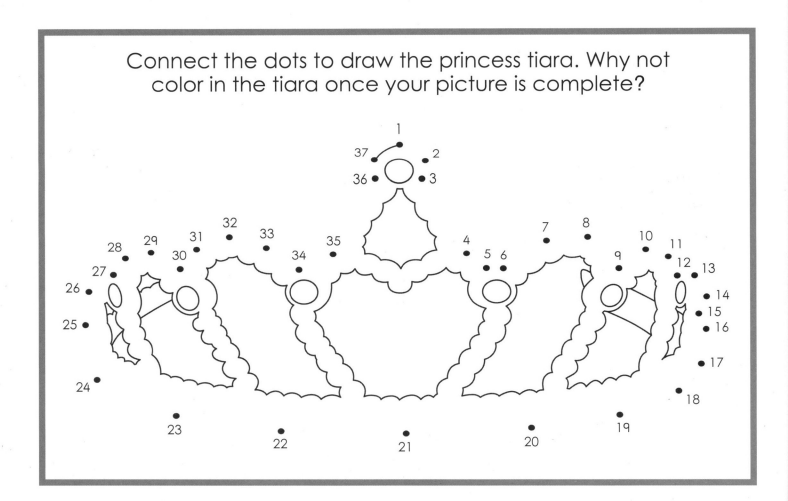

Today is Smokey the dragon's birthday. Do you know how old he is? Count the candles on his cake and write your answer in the box.

Can you find **five** shiny keys, **four** green toads, **three** blue potions, **two** hairy spiders, and **one** wizard hat? Circle the objects when you find them.

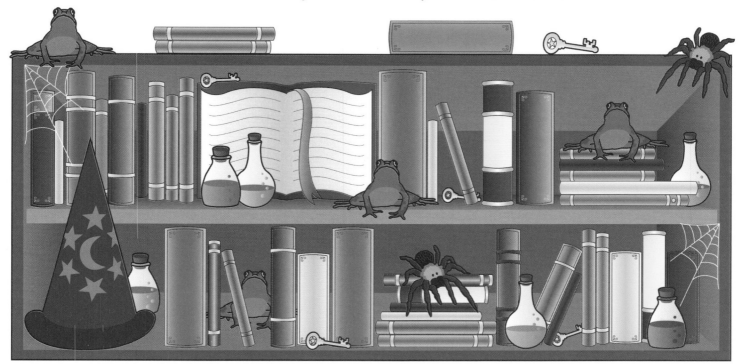

When is your next birthday? How old will you be?

Fill in the numbers 1, 2, 3, or 4 into the empty squares. Each number must appear once in each row, column, and box of four squares.

Puzzle 1:

	4		3
3	2		1
4		1	
	1		4

Puzzle 2:

	1	3	4
3			
	3	2	1
1			3

Puzzle 3:

1		4	2
2			1
4		2	
3			4

Puzzle 4:

2		3	
	4		2
		3	
1	2	4	

If you need help with the puzzles, turn back to the first sudoku page.

Add together the numbers on the first two soccer shirts.
Write your answer on the blank shirt.

3 + 4 =

Matching numbers

Count each group of soccer things, trace over the numbers, and then draw a line to the groups they match.

4

3

2

5

Can you think of any other soccer things?

Look closely at the stable scene, and then answer the counting questions.

How many horseshoes can you count?

How many carrots can you count?

How many ponies are in the field?

How many yellow ribbons are there?

How many trophies can you find in the scene?

Can you find all the objects in the bedroom scene?

1 cozy bed 2 mirrors

3 strawberries 4 lamps

8 pink socks

7 apples

6 clocks 5 blue chairs

Do you have any of these things in your bedroom?

Follow the instructions to complete the number pictures.

Draw two wheels on the car.

Add five spots to the dice.

Draw six whiskers on the kitten.

Add three more flowers to the bunch.

What shape are the wheels on the car?

When you halve a number, the amount you subtract is equal to the number that is left over. Follow the instructions below to find the answers.

Cross out the dolls to make **half of 4.**

   =

Cross out the ducks to make **half of 6.**

 =

Cross out the toy soldiers to make **half of 8.**

 =

How many buttons?

Circle the teddy bear that has the most buttons.

Do you have any of these toys?

Can you find all the objects in the seaside scene?

1 sand castle 2 boats

3 seagulls 4 starfish

7 shells 8 coconuts

6 crabs 5 palm trees

Draw the correct number of dots on the blank dominoes. Each domino should have the same number of dots as the one beside it. An example has been done to help you.

Count the numbers and write your answers in the boxes below.

5 9 7
9 7 9
7 9 5

How many number 5s are there?	
How many number 7s?	
How many number 9s?	

Which domino is the color pink?

Subtract the first group from the second group, and then write the answers in the boxes.

▬ means "subtract"

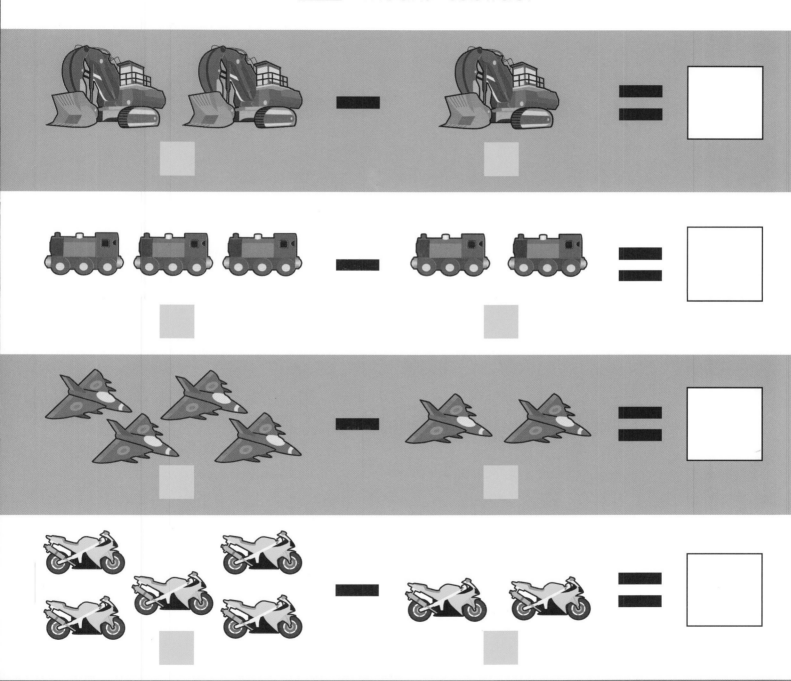

Which machine digs up dirt and rocks?

Connect the dots to draw the big rig. Why not color in the scene once your picture is complete?

Fast cars

Write the number on the last race car to complete the number pattern.

2   4   6

Who drives a race car?

How many bones can you find in the scene?
Write your answer in the box.

Triceratops used its horns as a defense against predators. How many horns does Triceratops have? Circle your answer below.

| 5 | 4 | 6 | 3 |

How many trees can you count in the prehistoric scene?

Fill in the numbers 1, 2, 3, or 4 into the empty squares. Each number must appear once in each row, column, and box of four squares.

1	3	2	4
			3
2		3	
3	1		2

3	4		1
2		3	
	2		3
4		1	2

	3	1	
1		3	4
2	1		3
	4	2	

1			3
2	3		4
3		4	2
	2	3	

If you need help with the puzzles, turn back to the first sudoku page.

Count all the space things, and then write your answers in the boxes.

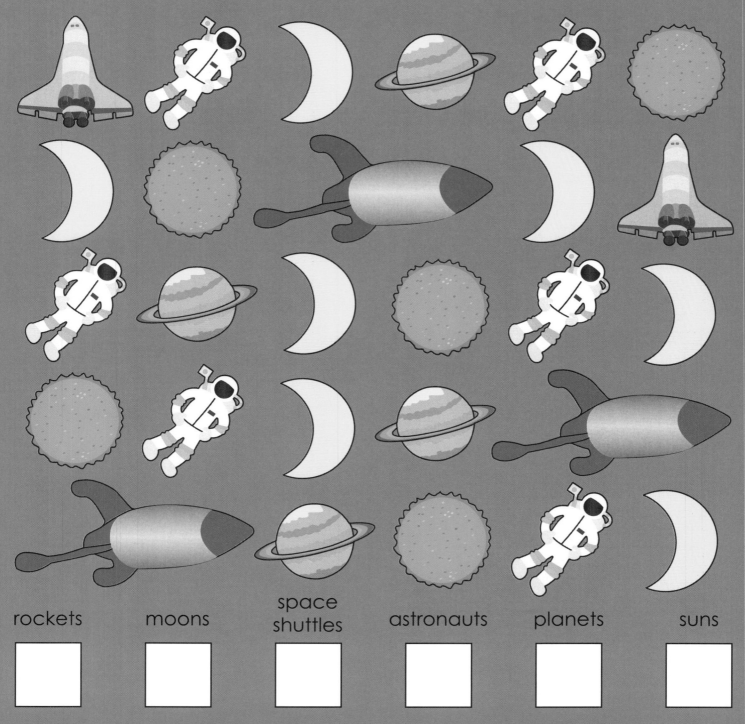

rockets	moons	space shuttles	astronauts	planets	suns

What shape is the moon?

Look at the flag of the United States. Count the different colored stripes, and then circle your answers below.

red
stripes

| 7 | 9 |

white
stripes

| 5 | 6 |

Connect the dots to draw the Sydney Opera House.
Why not color in the scene once your picture is complete?

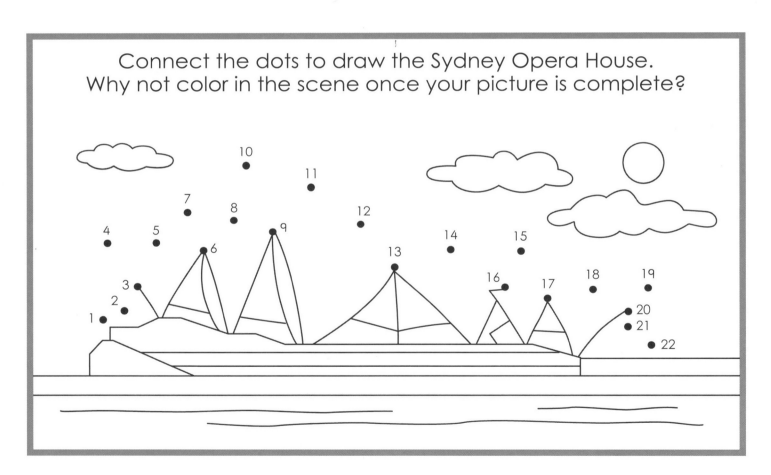

How many stars are there on the United States flag?

How many black spots does the ladybug have? Circle your answer below.

| 5 | 2 | 6 | 3 |

On the rock

Circle the bug that has eight legs.

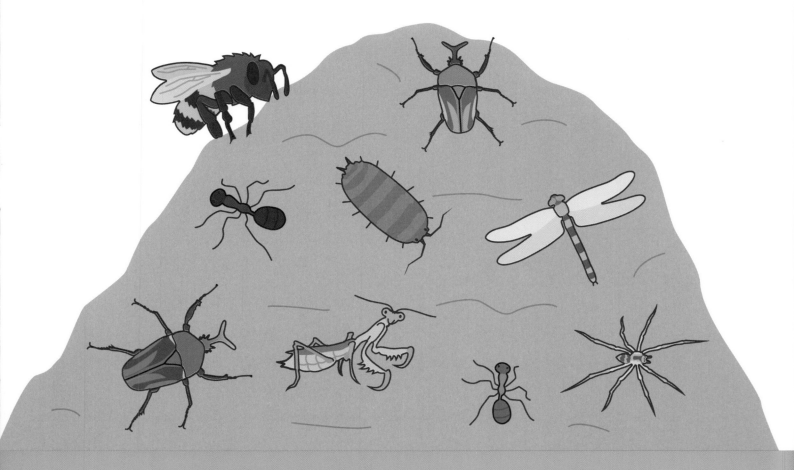

How many of these bugs have you seen before?

Can you find all the objects in the yard scene?

1 swing 2 rain boots

3 cats 4 watering cans

8 butterflies

7 worms

6 red flowers 5 birds

In what kind of weather do you wear rain boots?

Count all the pets, and then write the totals in the boxes.

puppies	goldfish	turtles	rabbits	guinea pigs	mice

Which pet has fins?

Connect the dots to draw the sailfish. Why not color in the ocean scene once your picture is complete?

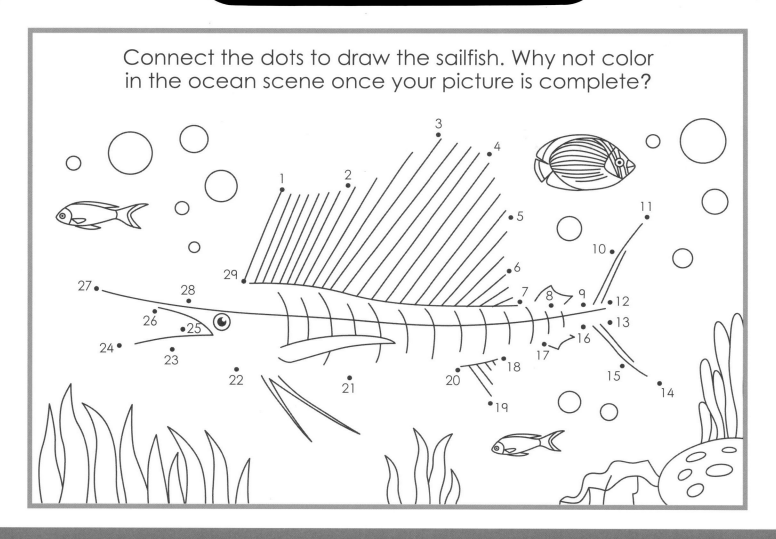

Amazing starfish

Some starfish can have as many as 50 arms. How many arms does this starfish have? Circle your answer below.

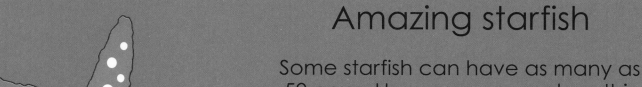

| 3 | 6 | 4 | 5 |

Do you know a sea creature that has eight arms?

Which group has the most giraffes? Circle your answer.

On the plain

How many zebras can you find on the African plain?
Write your answer in the box.

Which animal has horns and which animal has tusks?

Add the first group to the second group, and then write the totals in the boxes.

= means "equals"

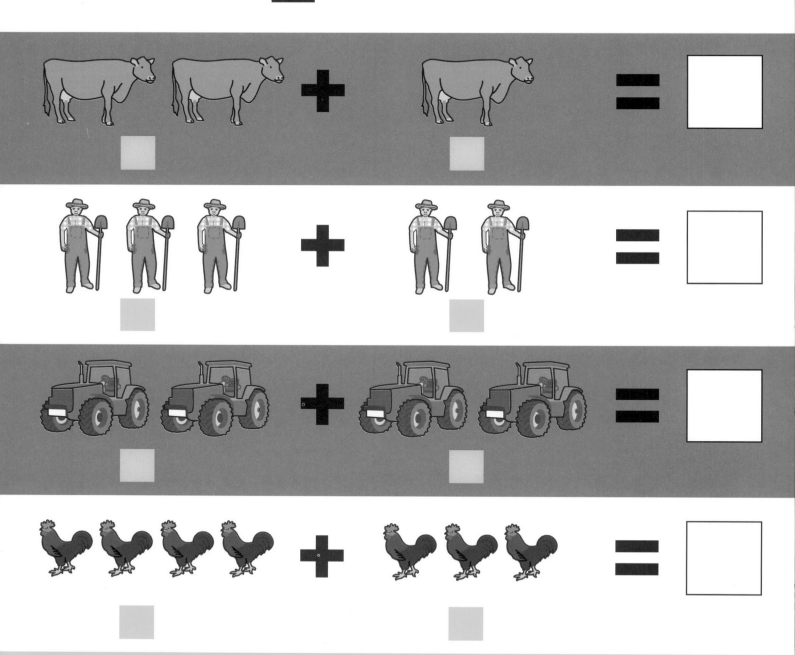

How many more farmers are there than tractors?

Count each animal group and write the totals in the boxes below.
Can you also answer the questions?

Farm babies

Which farm baby is pink?
Circle your answer above.

At the poles

Which animal has wings?
Circle your answer above.

Under the sea

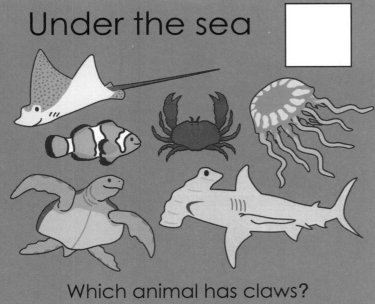

Which animal has claws?
Circle your answer above.

Jungle animals

Which animal has stripes?
Circle your answer above.

Have you ever seen any of these animals?

Count the number of sides each shape has, trace over the numbers, and then draw a line to the shape they match.

How many stars can you see in the sky? Circle your answer below.

3

8

4

5

8

7

10

9

Do you know the name of the shape with the most sides?

Fill in the numbers 1, 2, 3, or 4 into the empty squares. Each number must appear once in each row, column, and box of four squares.

Look at the example:

Now try these sudoku puzzles.

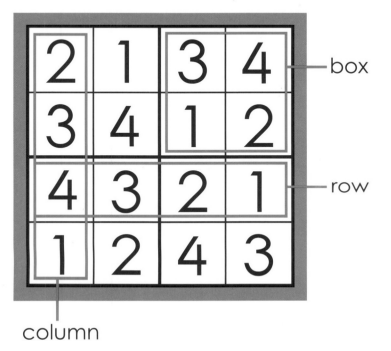

box

row

column

2	1	3	4
3	4	1	2
4	3	2	1
1	2	4	3

2		1	4
1	4		3
	1		2
4	2		1

1		3	2
3	2		
4		2	
	3	4	1

	2		1
3		2	4
1	3		2
2		1	3

Circle all the number 3s on the page.

Count the objects and write your answers in the boxes.

How many yellow things can you count? ☐

How many things are not green? ☐

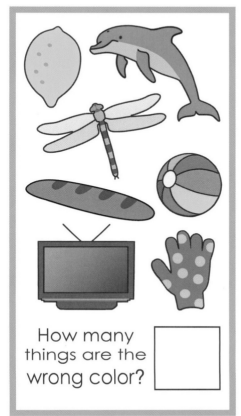

How many things are the wrong color? ☐

Rainbow colors

Count the number of colors in the rainbow, and then circle your answer.

8   6   7   9

Can you name all the colors in the rainbow?

Add the two groups of peas together, and then draw
the total number of peas in the boxes.

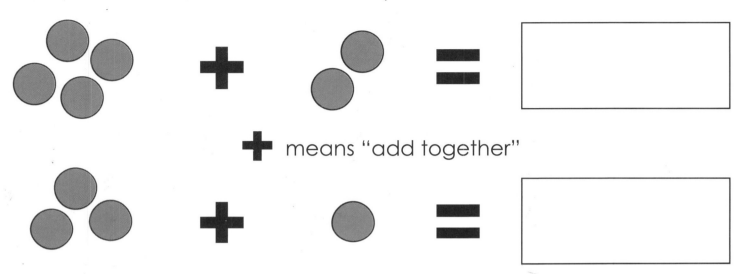

+ means "add together"

Can you find **six** bananas, **five** ice cream cones, **four** cupcakes,
three sandwiches, **two** slices of melon, and **one** slice of orange?

A banana is a fruit. Can you name any other fruits?